ABC
AND ME

Written by **Roda Ahmed**
Illustrated by **Fanny Liem**

is for

Baby

is for

Captain

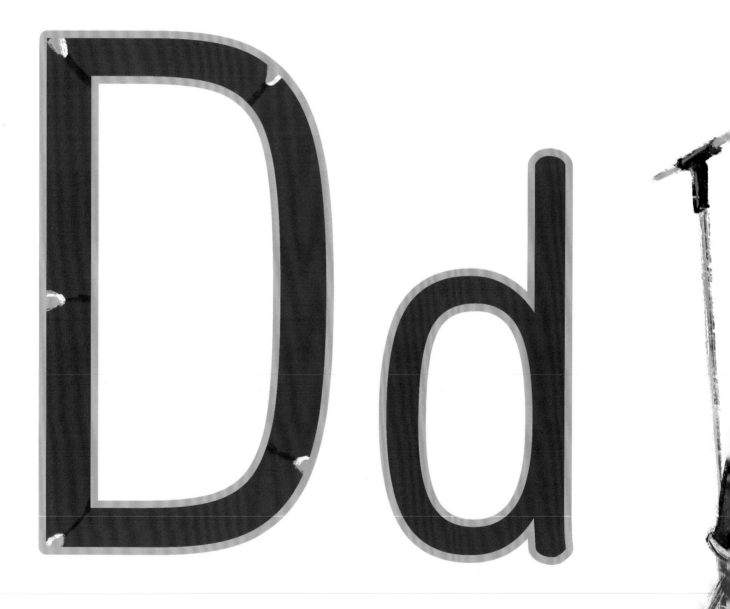

is for

Drums

is for

Elephant

is for
Family

is for
Grandpa

is for

Hair

is for

Ice cream

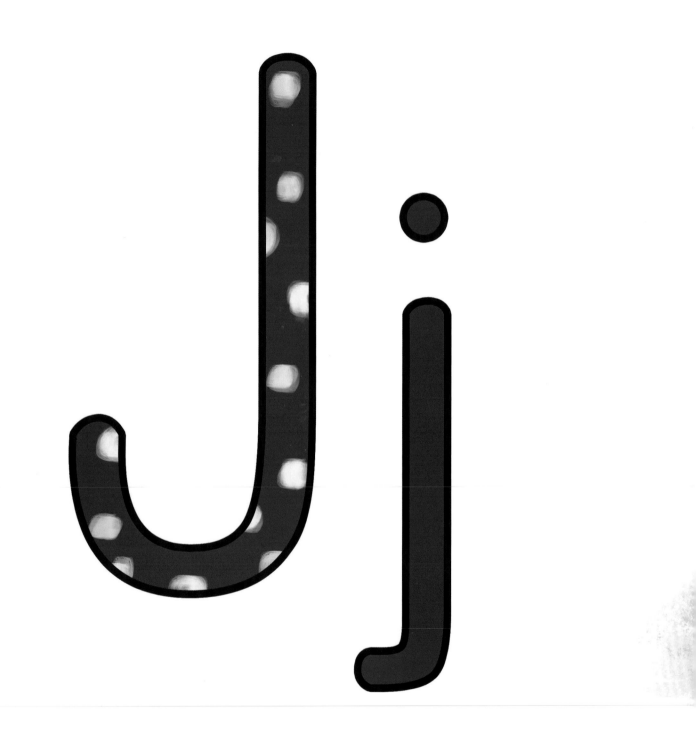

is for

Jump

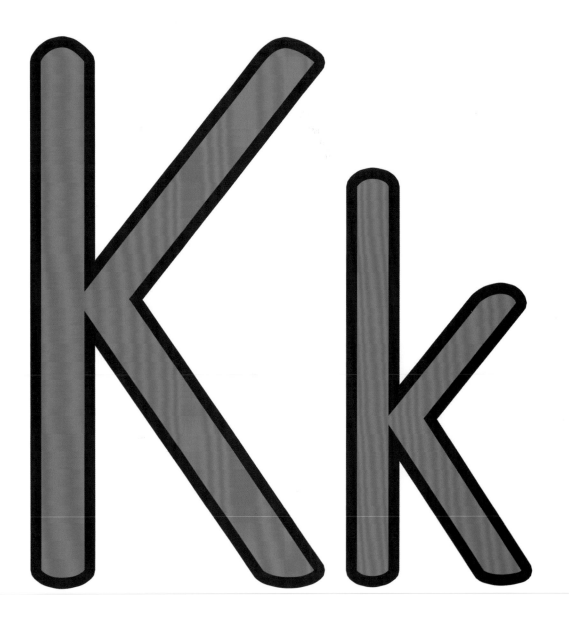

is for

King

is for
Love

is for

Moon

is for

Nose

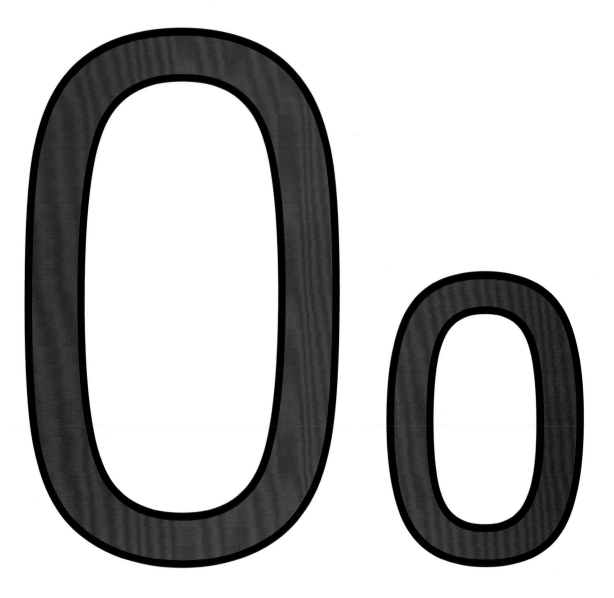

is for **Owl**

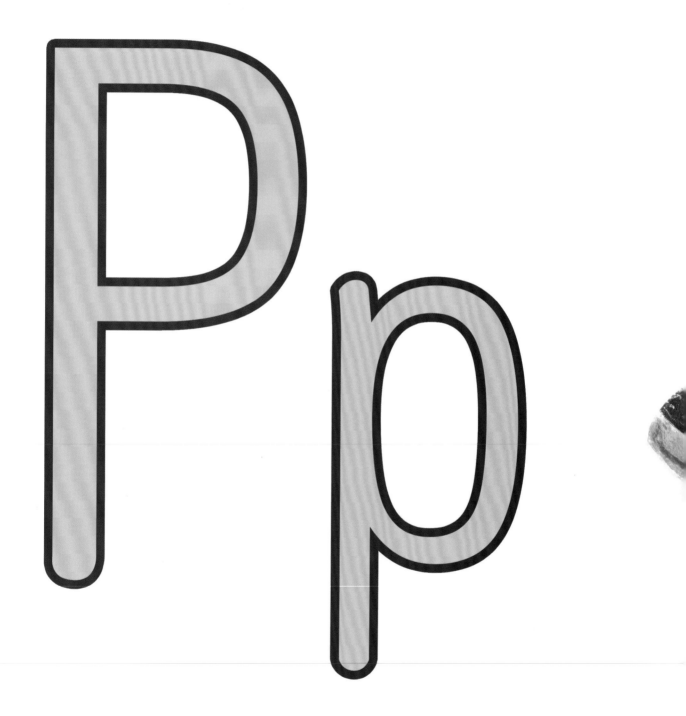

is for

Pilot

is for
Queen

is for

Rainbow

is for Son

is for

Tooth

is for **Us**

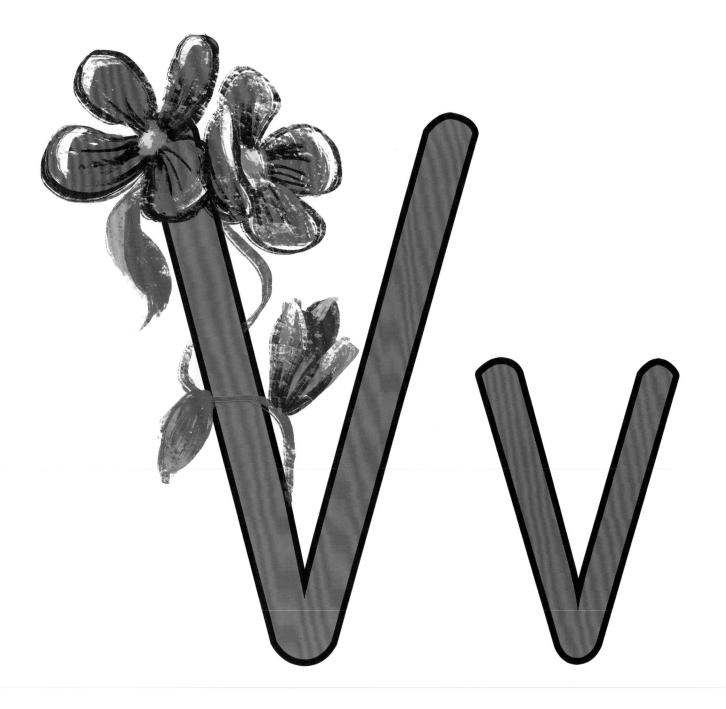

is for

Violet

is for Women

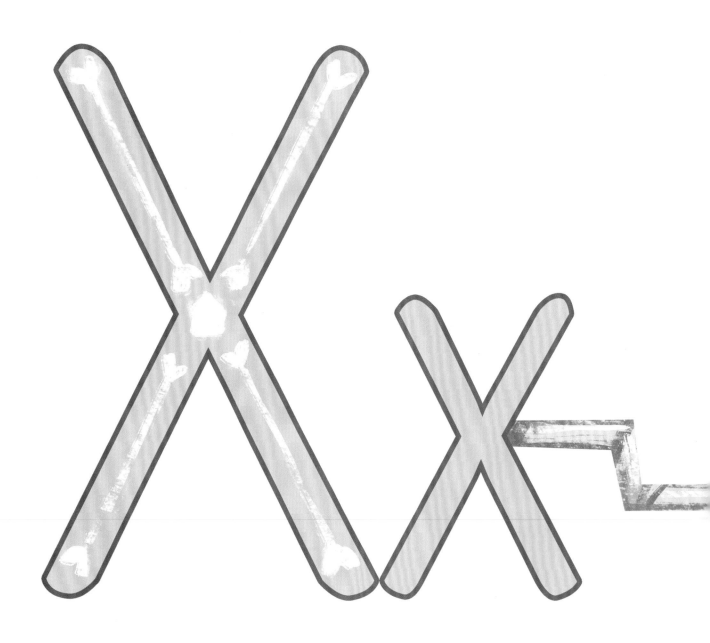

is for

X-ray

is for

You

is for

Zebra